This book belongs to

. . . .

Retold by Ronne Randall
Illustrated by Anna C. Leplar

This is a Parragon Publishing book
First published in 2005

Parragon Publishing
Queen Street House
4 Queen Street
Bath BA1 1HE, UK

Copyright © Parragon 2005

ISBN 1-40544-782-6

Printed in Indonesia

The Grimm Brothers
Cinderella

p

Once upon a time there was a pretty young girl who lived alone with her father, because, sadly, the girl's mother had died when she was a baby.

As the years passed, her father decided she needed a mother. So he got married again. The girl was excited, for her new stepmother had two daughters of her own, and she looked forward to having stepsisters.

But the stepmother was unkind, and the stepsisters were mean. The girl, who was a gentle, happy child, did her best to get along with them anyway.

Then, one day, the girl's stepmother said to her, "You must help with the housework."

So every day, the girl got up at dawn to cook and clean and wash and sew for her stepmother and stepsisters. Soon the girl's pretty clothes were in rags and tatters, and she was not allowed any new ones.

Not long after, her stepmother said to the girl, "Since you spend so much time in the kitchen, you can sleep beside the fire."

So every night she curled up to sleep beside the fire. Soon her clothes and hair were so gray with ashes and cinders that everyone called her Cinderella.

One morning, a messenger came to the house with a special invitation. There was to be a ball at the royal palace. All the young women in the kingdom were invited so that the young prince could choose a bride.

Cinderella's stepsisters were so excited. "We must look our best!" they cried.

"Cinderella! Comb my hair!" shouted one stepsister.

"Cinderella! Lace my dress!" ordered the other.

"Cinderella! Bring my jewels!"

"Cinderella! Get my shoes!"

When they were dressed, the two stepsisters admired themselves in the mirror. Cinderella watched and sighed. She wished she could go to the ball, too.

As an elegant carriage took her stepsisters to the ball, Cinderella sat beside the hearth and wept.

"How I wish I could go to the ball," she cried.

Suddenly, a strange light filled the room.

"Dry your tears, my dear," said a gentle voice.

Cinderella looked up. A golden glow surrounded a kind-looking woman with a glittering wand.

"Who are you?" asked Cinderella, blinking in wonder.

"I am your fairy godmother," she replied. "I have come to help you go to the ball."

"But how?" asked Cinderella.

"I will show you," said her fairy godmother, leading her out to the garden.

"Find me a big pumpkin, six white mice, six frogs, and a rat," said the fairy godmother.

Cinderella found everything as quickly as she could.

The fairy godmother tapped the pumpkin with her wand. Before Cinderella's eyes, the pumpkin changed into a magnificent golden coach.

Next, the fairy godmother waved her wand over the six white mice. A shower of sparks lit the air, and suddenly, instead of mice, six prancing horses stood before Cinderella.

"Ohhh!" she breathed in delight.

Then, with a gentle tap of her wand, the fairy godmother changed the six frogs into handsome footmen dressed in green velvet jackets. One more tap, and the rat became a fine coachman.

Cinderella was amazed. But still something was not right.

"What about my ragged clothes?" she asked.

Her fairy godmother answered with a gentle tap of her wand. Instantly, Cinderella's dusty dress became a shimmering ball gown, twinkling with jewels. On her feet were two sparkling glass slippers.

"Thank you!" gasped Cinderella with delight.

"Now," said her fairy godmother, "you are ready for the ball. But remember this: you must be home before midnight. At the stroke of midnight the magic will end, and everything will change back to what it was."

"I will remember," promised Cinderella as she stepped into the golden carriage.

16

When Cinderella arrived at the ball, everyone turned to look at her. No one knew who Cinderella was. Even her own stepsisters didn't recognize the beautiful girl in the dazzling gown.

But the prince thought that she was the loveliest, most enchanting girl he had ever seen. He never left her side, and danced only with her. Before the evening was over, he was in love with her.

Cinderella was falling in love with the prince, too. As she whirled around the room in his arms, Cinderella felt so happy that she forgot her fairy godmother's warning.

All at once, she heard the clock chime—once, twice… twelve times!

"Oh!" cried Cinderella. "I must go!" And before the prince could stop her, she ran from the ballroom and out of the palace.

"Wait!" cried the prince, dashing after her. But by the time he reached the palace steps, the mysterious girl had disappeared. All he could see was a ragged kitchen maid hurrying toward the palace gates.

But then he saw something twinkling on the steps— a single glass slipper. The prince picked it up.

"This will help me find her!" he said.

The next morning, the prince made an announcement.

"I will marry the woman whose foot fits the glass slipper," he declared. "I will search the kingdom until I find her."

That very day, he began going from house to house, looking for his true love. Every young woman in the kingdom tried on the glass slipper, but it didn't fit anyone.

At last the prince came to Cinderella's house. Her stepsisters were waiting to try on the slipper.

The first stepsister pushed and squeezed, but she could barely get her fat toes into the tiny slipper.

The second stepsister's feet were even bigger. But she too tried to cram her foot into the dainty little shoe.

It was no use.

The prince was turning to leave when a soft voice asked, "May I try the slipper, please?"

As Cinderella stepped forward to try on the slipper, her stepsisters began to laugh and make fun of her.

"Get back to the kitchen where you belong!" ordered her stepmother.

But the prince stepped forward.

"Everyone should have a chance," he said gently, "even a kitchen maid. Please," he said to Cinderella, "try on the slipper."

Cinderella sat down and took off her rough wooden clogs. The prince held out the sparkling slipper. And suddenly...

"Oh!" gasped her stepsisters.

"Oh my!" choked her stepmother.

For, of course, Cinderella's dainty foot fitted into the slipper perfectly.

As her stepsisters gazed in amazement, the prince joyfully took Cinderella in his arms.

"You are my one true love," the prince said to Cinderella. "Will you be my bride?"

"Yes," said Cinderella, with shining eyes.

Her stepsisters and stepmother were still trembling with shock as they watched Cinderella ride off to the palace in the prince's own carriage.

Cinderella and the prince were soon married, and because Cinderella was good and kind, she invited her stepsisters and stepmother to the wedding. They were never unkind again, and Cinderella and the prince lived happily ever after.

The End